Katie
and Those Boys

Other Apple Paperbacks by
MARTHA TOLLES:

and Those Boys

Original title: *Too Many Boys*

Martha Tolles

AN
APPLE
PAPERBACK

SCHOLASTIC INC.
New York Toronto London Auckland Sydney

ISBN 0–590–41794–0

Copyright © 1974, 1965 by Martha Tolles. All rights reserved. Published by Scholastic Inc., by arrangement with the author. APPLE PAPER-BACKS is a registered trademark of Scholastic Inc.

12 11 10 9 8 7 6 5 4 3   9/8 0 1 2 3/9

Printed in the U.S.A.   11

First Scholastic printing, June 1988

To My Mother

The Secret

It was early Saturday morning and Apple Street, with its neighborhood of boys, was still quiet. Katie Hart hurried outside and turned on the hose to water her garden behind the garage. She had planted it herself, and she looked with satisfaction at the even green rows of radishes, carrots, and tomatoes.

She was humming quietly as she sprinkled the plants, when suddenly she heard a rustling in the hedge between her house and the Madisons' house, next door. Who was that, so early in the morning? Not one of her brothers. It took Jamie half an hour to tie his shoes, and Dick wouldn't be up yet, not on a Saturday. The bushes shook again and then a big clod of dirt came sailing over the hedge and landed, plop, right in her garden. Katie didn't have to wonder who it was any longer — she knew.

"Will Madison!" she said indignantly, brushing the dirt off the plants. "You stop that! You almost

1

ruined my vegetables." But there was no answer. That made Katie even angrier. He could at least say something, she thought. Katie was just about to tell him so, when she had a better idea. She turned quietly toward the bushes and at the same time turned up the nozzle of the hose and squirted at the rustling place in the hedge. The bushes shook wildly, and there was a furious sputtering.

"All right for you, Katie Hart!" Will shouted. "I didn't hurt your old garden. I'm going to get you for this." Katie saw Will run up the back steps and into his house.

Will Madison, the biggest pest in the whole fifth grade, was soaking wet. For once Katie had gotten even with old freckle-nose Will for all the times he'd teased her, and shot rubber bands at her, and called her Goody Two-Shoes. She wondered a little uneasily, though, just how *he* would get even with her.

Katie put away the hose and walked around to the front yard. All the lawns up and down Apple Street looked smooth and green, except for her yard and the Madisons'. These two had a used look about them, because all the boys in the neighborhood gathered here in the afternoons for ball games, wrestling matches, snake-in-the-grass, and hide-and-go-seek.

Katie looked at the worn patches and sighed a

little to herself. If only there weren't so many boys on Apple Street! There were plenty of friends for Jamie and Dick, but none at all for Katie. She looked at the trim green lawn on the other side of her house. It belonged to Mr. Johnson, and it was carefully tended by a gardener. One of Katie's favorite places to play was the summer house in Mr. Johnson's garden. It was a wonderful place to have a picnic. Thinking of food reminded Katie that she hadn't had breakfast yet, and she hurried indoors.

The Harts's large dining room looked cool and inviting, with its leafy green wallpaper and big window looking out on Apple Street.

"Will Madison just threw dirt in my garden," Katie announced, sitting down next to Jamie, who went right on eating as if he hadn't heard her. He held his pet toad, Wilbur, in a box on his knees. Katie's father didn't even look up from his newspaper, and her mother only murmured, "That's too bad, dear."

"Will's all right," Katie's tall teenaged brother Dick said as he came into the room. "He wouldn't hurt anything."

"You always stick up for him," Katie protested. "I think he's a big pest. I wish there were some girls around here." Katie had lots of friends at school of course — Sarah Lou and Jody, Sue and

Mary — but Apple Street was at the edge of town. It was a long way to come after school, even on a bike.

"Girls!" echoed Jamie. "What good are girls?"

"Girls!" grinned Dick, picking up the sports page.

"They're a lot better than boys, Jamie Hart," Katie exclaimed. "I just wish you and those friends of yours — "

"Katie, Jamie," Mr. Hart said behind his paper, "stop arguing, please." Katie stared unhappily at her plate. As usual, she hadn't gotten much sympathy from her family about her troubles with Will Madison. How much nicer it must be for Sarah Lou, with two sisters — and Jody too. Jody lived near Sarah Lou and she was always at her house. But here at home Katie was always having to stay out of the boys' way when they played games. And they hardly ever asked her to play with them.

"Katie, would you like to hold Wilbur after breakfast?" Jamie asked suddenly. Katie smiled a little. Jamie was trying to make up, she knew. He considered it a real treat to hold Wilbur.

"Never mind, Katie," Mrs. Hart said soothingly. "Maybe things will improve. In fact, I know something. . . ."

Katie looked questioningly at her mother.

"I can't tell you yet," Mrs. Hart went on, "but it might make things better for you."

"What is it, Mother?" Katie asked eagerly. But Mrs. Hart just smiled and shook her head.

Just then the telephone rang. Dick went to answer it, and in a moment he was back, towering over the table excitedly.

"Pop!" he shouted. "The man says I can have it for only eighty dollars. What do you say, Pop? I've got the money." Mr. Hart folded his paper slowly and looked at his son, who was almost as tall as he was.

"All right, Dick," he said. "Your mother and I talked it over last night."

"Yahooo," Dick yelled with delight and hurried back to the telephone.

"Have what?" Jamie demanded.

"It's an old car that doesn't run," Mrs. Hart explained. "At least, not yet, thank goodness."

"Boy, oh boy!" exclaimed Dick, dashing back into the dining room. "It's coming Thursday afternoon."

"What good is a car that can't run?" Jamie asked.

"I'm going to fix it up so it *can* run." Dick grinned. "I'll work on it in the backyard."

"Not near my garden, I hope," Katie said anxiously.

"No. I won't hurt your old garden," Dick said, giving Katie's long brown hair a tug.

After breakfast Katie went out in the front yard with Jamie, but he soon trotted off to find his friend Bobby Carson. Katie was just going back into the house to call Sarah Lou when Will Madison came whizzing along the sidewalk on his bike.

"Yahooo," he yelled. "There's that mean old Katie Hart."

"Will Madison . . ." Katie began.

"I'm going to get even with you, Katie Hart. You'll see."

As she stood looking at him, Katie couldn't help worrying about what he might do. How in the world could her mother say things might get better when a boy like Will Madison lived next door!

The Car

On Thursday afternoon Dick's car arrived. A tow truck pulled it up to the house, then Dick and his friends from high school pushed the car into the backyard. There was Ed Ferguson, Bob Potter, who had his Irish setter with him, and Charlie Davis. Of course Will Madison had to come over with his friend Short Stuff.

Katie watched them pushing the car down the drive. Every time she looked at Will, Katie got an uneasy feeling. Not only had she soaked him with the hose on Saturday, but that very day she had gotten him into trouble at school. In English class he threw an eraser and it almost hit their teacher, Miss Pratt, as she walked into the room. When she asked who had thrown the eraser, Katie told and Miss Pratt made Will stay in during the noon recess.

Thinking about it now made Katie uncomfortable. She wished she hadn't said anything. She really hadn't meant to. It just popped out before she had a chance to think. It seemed as if she was getting deeper and deeper in trouble with Will Madison.

The boys were thrilled with the car. One minute they had the hood up, looking at the engine, the next they were flat on their backs underneath the car. Even Jamie examined it. And when Mr. Hart came home from work he joined the boys.

"That old thing will never be any good," Katie said loudly as she watched the boys crowded around the engine. They turned and stared at her in surprise.

"You don't know a good car when you see one!" exclaimed Short Stuff.

"I don't see what's so good about it." Katie tossed her head. "And please don't step on my garden."

"Please don't step on my garden," a high voice mimicked her. All the boys laughed at Will's imitation.

"Hey, look at this!" Dick called from under the hood. The boys closed in around the car again and forgot all about Katie.

The next afternoon Sarah Lou visited Katie. Since she didn't come very often, Katie tried to think of something special and exciting to do. Dick and his friends were in a ball game at school, so she suggested to Sarah Lou that they play in Dick's car.

"Oh, that's a good idea!" Sarah Lou exclaimed. "We can pretend we're old-fashioned ladies out driving. And let's take something along to eat." Sarah Lou was always hungry.

Katie got some cookies out of the kitchen and the girls hurried out to the car. They sat on the back seat nibbling cookies and pretending they were being chauffeured on a shopping trip.

"Do you think this car will ever really run?" Sarah Lou asked.

"I don't know," Katie said doubtfully, looking at all the greasy car parts laid out in neat piles on the lawn. "Dick thinks he will have it running by the time he gets his driver's license in the fall."

The girls were having so much fun that they lost all track of time. Suddenly Dick was standing beside the car.

"Come on, girls, time to get out," he said. Katie could tell he was pleased they were enjoying his car. "I have to get to work on this thing now. This way, ladies," he said, opening the door.

Sarah Lou giggled. Sarah Lou always giggled around boys. That was probably because she wasn't around them very much, Katie thought.

"What do you think of my fine car?" Dick asked.

"It's fun to play in," Sarah Lou said. "Can we have a ride in it if you ever get it fixed?"

"Oh, I'll get it fixed. Don't worry," Dick said.

Dick could do lots of things, and his plans often

turned out well. He was usually too busy to pay much attention to Katie, but every once in a while he would teach her a new card game, and he already had taught her how to dance a little.

"Come on, now," Dick went on. "I have to get to work."

As the girls passed the garage, Katie noticed her garden for the first time that day.

"My garden!" she cried. "Who did that to my garden?" It was a mess. The neat rows of plants had been torn up. The tiny carrot and onion plants were lying about, and some of the tomato plants had been torn from their stakes and trampled into the ground. "Who could have done it?" Katie wailed.

"Oh, what a shame, Katie. Your nice garden!" Sarah Lou tried to comfort her friend.

"Say, that's really a mess," Dick said, coming over to the girls.

Katie turned to her brother. "Do you know how it happened?" she asked. But she knew he didn't, or he would have told her. Maybe Jamie, Katie thought, though it seemed too mean a thing for Jamie to do. Besides, he was interested in the garden too; he helped her weed and water it sometimes. Then Katie remembered Will's threats to get even with her and how she had gotten him in trouble in school.

"I'll bet it was that Will Madison!" Katie burst out.

"Yes, that's probably who it was, Katie," Sarah Lou agreed, slipping her arm around Katie's waist.

"Now, Katie, you don't know that. Will — "

"I certainly do," Katie interrupted her brother. "He's the worst pest — and I'm going to speak to him right now." With this she and Sarah Lou marched off to look for Will. It wasn't long before they saw him riding up Apple Street on his bike, a pack of books slung on his back. He was whistling loudly.

"There's Goody Two-Shoes," he jeered when he saw Katie. Katie ignored the taunt.

"Will Madison," she said in a loud voice. "What's the idea of tearing up my garden?"

Will slowed his bike and stared at her. "What?" he said.

"Yes," Sarah Lou added. "Why did you have to ruin all those vegetables?"

"What are you talking about?"

"Oh, don't put on such an act," Katie said indignantly. "We know you did it. My garden is a mess. It's all torn up."

"Well, why blame me?" Will scowled at her.

"Who else could have done it?" Katie demanded.

11

"How should I know?" Will shouted angrily. "I don't know anything about your old garden. So there!" And he rode off.

"I still think he did it," Katie said to Sarah Lou, and her friend agreed.

Katie told the rest of her family about the garden later that day. They were sympathetic and Jamie offered to help her fix it. But when Katie asked her mother, "Are you going to speak to Mrs. Madison?" Dick protested. "Will says he didn't do it," Dick insisted. "And you didn't see him do it."

"But he must have," Katie said stubbornly. "And I think he should be punished."

"Now, Katie," her father said, "it's not right to accuse people unless you can prove it."

"Your father's right, Katie," her mother said. "There's no way of telling *who* tore up your garden."

But Katie was convinced it was Will Madison and she felt furious with him for it.

New Buyers

About a week later, at breakfast, Mrs. Hart made an announcement.

"Mr. Johnson," she said, "has decided to sell his house and move to Redingford to be near his daughter. That's the secret," she said to Katie.

"The secret!" Katie echoed. "But I like Mr. Johnson. I don't want him to move away." Katie felt disappointed, and she couldn't see how this was going to be good for her.

"He'll be much better off in an apartment," Mrs. Hart went on. "That house is too much for him to keep up. And don't you see, Katie? We'll be getting new neighbors."

Katie put down her fork and looked at her mother. She hadn't thought about new neighbors. "Why, maybe it will be a family with a girl!" she exclaimed.

"Maybe." Her mother smiled.

"Maybe boys," Dick said, teasing Katie.

Now Katie understood why her mother had

said it *might* turn out to be a good thing for Katie. It all depended on the new neighbors.

That very morning a "For Sale" sign was put up on Mr. Johnson's lawn by the Blackstone Realtors. It wasn't long before people started coming to look at the property.

Katie sat on the front steps of her house and stared longingly at them, wondering if they had any daughters. Maybe a whole family of girls would move in. Sarah Lou had Jody living near her, and Mary had Sue. Now maybe it was Katie's turn.

Katie went around to her garden and watered the vegetable plants that she had carefully replanted and tied up the night before. They still had a wilted look, but with good care she hoped they would be all right. She smoothed the soil again and pulled out a few weeds. That Will! He was just the meanest boy.

Dick came out and started to work on his car. When Bob arrived with Charlie and some more of Dick's friends, Katie decided to go back into the house. She was walking toward the back door when Will came around the corner of the house into the backyard.

Katie looked right past him and kept on walking.

"Katie, wait, please," Will called. But she continued up the back steps and slammed the door behind her. She would never speak to him again, ever, she decided, as she climbed the stairs to her room.

The next morning — Sunday — the Harts's doorbell rang very early. Only Katie and Jamie were up. When Katie answered the door, she was surprised to find a woman with four boys standing on the porch.

"My but you have a lovely house," the woman cooed.

"Why thank you," Katie responded, staring at the boys and wondering who they were.

"Do you mind if we come in? My name is Mrs. Walters." The woman smiled. "Come, boys," she went on, "be sure you wipe your feet. Such a lovely living room. Where is your mother, dear?" Mrs. Walters asked, as she stood in the hallway.

When Katie explained that the rest of her family was still in bed, Mrs. Walters said she was sorry to hear that.

"We'll just take a little look around down here then," the woman said. Katie was completely mystified.

"Can you manage things, then?" Mrs. Walters asked as she steered her four sons through the living room, dining room, and kitchen.

Katie nodded uncertainly, not sure just what was meant.

"Would you like to see my room?" Jamie asked. "I've got a great room."

"Thank you, dear, but we don't want to disturb anyone. We'll come back later," she added, to Katie's amazement.

Jamie offered to show the boys his toad and Dick's old car in the backyard.

"How very nice," Mrs. Walters murmured as Jamie conducted them around outside. "Well, thank you, my dears, for showing us around."

Katie walked around to the front of the house with the Walters and then she saw it — she should have guessed! There was the "For Sale" sign stuck smack in the middle of their own front lawn.

"Such a charming neighborhood for raising boys," Mrs. Walters said looking at the wide front lawn and the quiet street. "I suppose you're sorry to be moving."

"Oh, but we're not," Katie exclaimed.

"Really?" The woman looked startled.

"No, we're not. I don't know how that sign got over here," Katie said.

"Are you sure your house isn't for sale?" Mrs. Walters insisted. Katie shook her head.

"No, it's the one next door that's for sale. Someone put that sign over here for a joke."

"Well, I'm so sorry we bothered you," Mrs. Walters said, as she and the four boys walked off to their car. But she looked back at Katie as though she didn't know whether to believe her.

"Who do you suppose put that sign out there?" Jamie asked when he and Katie had returned to the kitchen.

Katie was wondering the same thing. It was the kind of trick some boy would play. Then she remembered how she had snubbed Will the day before when he had tried to speak to her. Of course, it was Will!

"I'm not sure, but I've got an idea who did it," Katie answered her brother.

"Then tell me," Jamie persisted.

"I can't till I'm sure. Now let's get that sign back before we have a whole string of people coming to see our house."

When her mother and father came down later that morning, Katie told them about the sign and the woman with the four boys. To her surprise, they laughed.

"Well, it was a good thing the house was clean," Mrs. Hart said.

"Well I think it was a terrible thing to do, moving that sign," Katie said and swept off to her room to get ready for Sunday School. She made her bed, pulling the corners tight, then straightened the books on the bookcase. She even dusted the glass figurines on her dresser. Katie liked to keep her room, which she and her mother had decorated in pink and white, neat and tidy.

At Sunday School Katie sat as far away from Will as she could. Once he turned and crossed his eyes at her. She looked away quickly.

As they left the church hall, Will came up behind her and said with a wicked grin, "I see you're selling your house."

"I *knew* you put that sign there!" Katie burst out.

Will just looked at her with big, innocent eyes. "Who? Me?" he said. "And I didn't tear up your old garden either," he called after her as she hurried out the door.

That afternoon Katie saw the Walters family return with the real estate agent. Before they left, they stood on the lawn of Mr. Johnson's house watching Dick and his friends play baseball in the street. Katie could just imagine Mrs. Walters saying again ". . . such a nice neighborhood for raising boys."

"Katie, guess what!" Jamie burst into Katie's room. "One of the Walters' boys told me they're going to buy Mr. Johnson's house."

"But they've only just seen it. I don't believe it," Katie wailed.

"He said so," Jamie insisted triumphantly. "He said his mother told him that after visiting our house, she decided she'd like to live next door to us."

Katie stared at her brother, not wanting to believe him.

"I guess moving that sign helped sell the house," Jamie added.

Katie's disappointment fed her anger toward Will Madison. It was his fault that four more boys were moving into the neighborhood. Maybe they never would have if the sign hadn't been moved, if they hadn't met Jamie and his toad, and seen Dick's car. Katie sank down on the edge of her bed and blinked back the tears.

"It's all right, Katie," Jamie said soothingly. "Look, here's Wilbur. Would you like to hold him for a little while?"

Troubles

What Jamie had told Katie about the Walters buying Mr. Johnson's house was true. The "For Sale" sign was taken down and a "Sold" sign went up in its place. Katie couldn't bear to look at it.

Then one day when she was coming home from school, she saw a moving van in front of Mr. Johnson's house. She stopped her bike to watch the movers carry out a big table and a rug. Then she heard one of the men say that Mr. Johnson would be leaving in a minute. Katie suddenly had an idea. She dropped her bike and ran around to her backyard to pick a bunch of lavender lilacs. As she hurried back, Mr. Johnson came out of his house, using a cane and leaning on his gardener's arm.

"These are for you," Katie said shyly, going up to the old man. "We're sorry you're leaving." Katie held out the flowers to Mr. Johnson.

"Why, thank you, Katie," Mr. Johnson smiled.

"That's right nice of you." He stood for a moment examining the flowers. Then he looked down at Katie. "You're growing tall, young lady. I remember you when you were just a bit of a thing."

Katie wondered why people always said they remembered you when you were small. But she realized Mr. Johnson must be sad at leaving the house where he had lived for so many years, and she smiled politely.

"Here, Katie," he added, taking out a business card. "This is my new address. Perhaps you wouldn't mind writing to me sometimes and telling me the news about Apple Street."

"All right, I will." Katie was pleased that he had asked her. "I hope you like your new apartment," she added.

"Thank you, my dear." Mr. Johnson walked slowly toward his car. "And I hope you like your new neighbors," he called back.

"I'll try," Katie said.

Mr. Johnson lowered himself carefully into the car, and the gardener went around to the driver's seat. As he started the engine, Mr. Johnson waved and said something Katie couldn't quite hear.

Katie waved until the car was out of sight, then she went into the house, and walked upstairs thoughtfully. But at the doorway of her room she stood staring in disbelief. Her doll collection was scattered all over the room. Her glass figurines were lying about on the floor, and a leg had been broken off her favorite glass horse. Even her jewelry box was lying open on the bed.

Katie was outraged. That Jamie! He must have done it! She found him out back, playing with his friend Bobby Carson.

"Jamie Hart," Katie shouted, rushing over to him. "You leave my things alone. Do you hear?" She gave his hair a yank.

"Ow, ow! Stop, Katie!" Jamie swung his fists at her, and Katie let him go, shouting, "You stay out of my room from now on, Jamie. And you too, Bobby."

"We were only playing," Jamie protested. "We didn't mean to hurt anything. Honest we didn't."

"Well, you did. You ruined my horse." Katie whirled around and went back upstairs to her room.

She sat down on the edge of the bed, close to tears. First her garden, and now her room. And four more boys were going to move in next door. It was too much.

During dinner Katie announced that she was never going to play cards or any other game with Jamie ever again. Jamie offered to help her tidy up, but Katie said she didn't want him in her room anymore.

"I'm sorry, Katie, honest I am," Jamie pleaded. But Katie wouldn't listen.

At bedtime she heard a knock on her door, and when she opened it, there was Jamie.

"Katie, did you see this keen purple rock I got? I'll let you have it."

"Go away," she said crossly, and shut the door.

But as she climbed into bed that night, Katie felt a little sorry she had been so angry with Jamie. When he had been a baby she had often helped her mother take care of him. Even now he would sometimes come to her instead of their mother when he had been hurt or had a problem. She closed her eyes and tried to forget about Jamie.

It was hours later when she was awakened by someone shaking her shoulder. It was Jamie.

"Katie," he whispered, "can I sleep in your other bed? I had an awful dream. It was scary. Please, Katie, can I?" Without waiting for an answer Jamie slid under the covers of the other twin bed in Katie's room.

"All right," Katie mumbled. She went back to sleep, feeling a little happier.

Haunted House

The news spread up and down Apple Street: The Walters weren't going to buy Mr. Johnson's house after all because Mr. Walters had been transferred to the West Coast.

Katie was thrilled. Now there was no telling what might happen. Maybe a whole family of girls would move in. But then the days passed and no one came near the house — no real estate agent and no buyer. It seemed as though the house had been forgotten by everyone but the Harts.

One Saturday Dick decided to mow Mr. Johnson's lawn. Katie helped him rake up the grass and weed some of the flower beds at the front of the house. When they finished, Katie went around to the back where the summerhouse stood in the center of a large formal rose garden. Gravel paths led off from the summerhouse like the spokes of a wheel, and the entire garden was enclosed by a high brick wall.

Katie entered the garden by a gate in the wall.

Now that the place was empty, what fun it would be if she and Sarah Lou could play here. Lately Sarah Lou was always going to visit Jody, or Jody was always going to visit Sarah Lou. But the summerhouse was quiet and away from all the boys and their noisy games that Sarah Lou found so annoying.

Katie hurried home to ask her mother if she and her friend could use the summerhouse to play in. Mrs. Hart said it would be all right if Katie and the girls picked up after they were through playing, and were careful not to damage anything.

That very afternoon Katie invited Sarah Lou to come over. The girls decided to make the summerhouse their clubhouse, and when the other girls in their class heard about their plans on Monday, they wanted to come over too. Katie suddenly had all the friends she could wish for. Jody, Sarah Lou, Mary, and Sue came every day. Now that the girls had a separate place to play the boys didn't bother them — not even Will Madison.

On Friday evening of that week Sarah Lou stayed for dinner at Katie's house. Since it was still light out after dinner, the girls went back to the summerhouse.

"I really like to come over to your house now, Katie," Sarah Lou said. "The boys aren't so bad anymore. They don't bother us the way they used to. When we're over here I guess they just don't think about us."

Katie smiled at her friend. A new girl hadn't moved in—maybe that would never happen—but at least no boys had moved in either. Nobody had. The girls had this place all to themselves. Katie could almost think kindly of Will, for in a way he had made this possible — if it was Will who had switched the sign. He still denied it.

Sarah Lou had no sooner mentioned boys than Jamie came into the garden. "Could I play with you, Katie?" he asked.

"Why don't you play with Bobby?" Sarah Lou asked.

"He can't play," Jamie said. "Please, Katie, can I?"

It had been quite awhile since Jamie had asked to play with her—more and more of the time now he trailed around after Dick.

"I guess so," Katie said. "If you don't mess up our clubhouse."

"And as long as you don't have that toad with you," Sarah Lou put in.

The girls had just gotten to sweeping out the summerhouse when they heard a shutter bang on one of the windows in Mr. Johnson's house.

"I wonder how that got loose," Katie said looking toward the house. "I never heard it before."

"What made it bang?" Sarah Lou asked. "There isn't any wind."

"No, there isn't," Katie said and felt a sudden chill in the early dusk as the shutter banged again. She watched it move slowly out from the side of the house and then fall back. There didn't seem to be any reason for it.

"I've got to feed Wilbur," Jamie said nervously and headed for the gate.

Katie stood still, staring at the house. "Oh — oh," she cried. "Look!" Something fluttered in the window. "Did you see it?" she cried to Sarah Lou.

"Yes, now it's in the other window!" screamed Sarah Lou. "Come on, let's get out of here."

"It's a ghost!" yelled Jamie and ran through the gate. Sarah Lou grabbed Katie and they streaked after him.

When they got home and told their story no one would believe them. The boys just laughed, and Mrs. Hart said it was nonsense, that it was probably just a trick of the twilight. There was no such thing as a ghost, she insisted. But she did send Dick over to look around the outside of the house. When he came back, he said he hadn't seen a thing — not a thing.

At school on Monday, the other girls in their class wouldn't believe Katie and Sarah Lou either. Jody and Sue and Mary laughed at the idea of a ghost and a haunted house on Apple Street.

"I don't believe a word of it," Jody said firmly.

"Me either," added Sue.

"Then come over this afternoon and maybe you can see for yourself," Katie said indignantly. She was tired of not being believed, and besides, it wouldn't be so scary in the summerhouse if they went in a big group. "Will you come too, Sarah Lou?"

"I guess so, if the others will," Sarah Lou said uncertainly. "But if that funny business starts again, I'm leaving."

That afternoon the five girls gathered in Mr. Johnson's backyard. At first they just stood around watching the house. After ten minutes, when nothing had happened, they decided to play school. But then, just as they were getting their school organized, the shutter on the house banged! The white "thing" floated across the upstairs windows and the shutter banged again. The girls huddled together, staring at the house.

"Let's go," cried Jody.

"I told you so," chorused Sarah Lou and Katie as they all raced across the garden.

Back at Katie's house they all talked at once — and this time Mrs. Hart listened carefully.

"I'm going over there myself, Katie," she said

when the girls had stopped talking. "Run; get Dick and ask the other boys if they'll come too."

In a few minutes Mrs. Hart, the girls, Dick, Bob Potter, Short Stuff, Will, and Jamie were standing in Mr. Johnson's backyard, looking at the upstairs windows of the house.

"Mother, you know how excited Katie gets," Dick protested. "How long do we have to wait around here to see if some crazy ghost will appear?"

"It's just girls' talk, Mrs. Hart," Short Stuff put in. "You can't believe everything they say. They mean to tell the truth but they exaggerate."

"But I saw it too," Jamie pointed out, "and I'm not a girl."

"I won't keep you long," Mrs. Hart assured them. "Let's just stand here and see what happens."

But nothing happened. Nothing at all. They stood and they waited. Will and Short Stuff teased the girls and said they had made it up to get attention. But the girls stuck to their story. When they went home that evening, they told Katie they weren't coming back to play in the summerhouse again.

Trapped

Since her friends wouldn't come to her house, Katie had to go to theirs. It was fun of course, but when she went to Sue's house, Mary was always there, and Jody was at Sarah Lou's house. They were such good friends that it gave Katie a left-out feeling. Sometimes it was hard for three of them to have a good time together. There would be one too many, and that one was usually Katie. The other girls liked her, Katie knew that, but they didn't need her.

One afternoon, when Jody had to go shopping after school with her mother, Sarah Lou agreed to go home with Katie. They decided to go by way of the creek that emptied into a lake about a mile beyond town. In summer, the lake was a busy place.

Along the creek there were moorings and docks for boats, but now the boats were tipped on the bank, covered with canvas, or riding at anchor in the water. Just where the creek emptied into the lake was a cluster of buildings. There was a building and dock for renting boats, a small lemonade stand, and a round little hut where sandwiches, soda, candy, and ice cream were sold. Sarah Lou and Katie walked slowly, looking at the boats, peering in the dusty windows of the hut. There was no one there now. It was deserted and it seemed as if the whole place belonged to them.

They circled the hut, where in summer they had to wait so long in line for soda and ice cream, and came upon a half-open window. Sarah Lou, who was walking ahead, turned and looked at Katie.

"Katie," she whispered, "let's go in."

"What for?" Katie asked. "And why are you whispering?"

"Well, I don't know," Sarah Lou answered, still in a whisper, "but come on, let's go in." Sarah Lou slid the window up and climbed through. "Come on," she urged. "There might be something to eat."

"I don't think we should do this." Katie hesitated, but it didn't seem right to let Sarah Lou go in alone so she climbed in after her. It was dark and musty in the stand, and not very tidy. It looked as though it had been closed up hastily at the end of the season. The display boxes of

31

candy were still partly filled with chocolate bars and gum, and half-filled cases of soda were scattered around the floor.

The girls stayed close together as they went slowly around the hut, stumbling against boxes and whispering "shhh" to each other.

"We could have a feast." Sarah Lou giggled. "Look at all this stuff," she said, scooping up a handful of candy bars.

"Mmmm, it does look good," Katie agreed, as she picked up several chocolate bars. The stand seemed so abandoned, the atmosphere so lonely, it was hard to believe the place belonged to anybody. Sarah Lou was right, they could have a feast. Suddenly Katie heard someone whistling outside.

"Sarah Lou," she whispered, clutching Sarah Lou's arm. "Who's that?"

They peered out through a boarded-up place over one of the windows, and there was Will Madison sauntering along the creek with his hands in his pockets.

"Not Will Madison!" wailed Katie. She ducked down out of sight and pulled Sarah Lou with her. "Good grief, what's he doing here? Now what will we do?"

Sarah Lou's eyes grew round with worry, and she shrugged her shoulders helplessly. Katie peeked out the window again after a few minutes.

She saw Will standing just a little way off on the dock. He had his back turned toward them, and he was skipping stones into the creek. Katie ducked down again quickly. "We can't get out with him there," she said angrily.

Sarah Lou nodded and looked more worried than ever. "What if he finds us here?" she said.

Katie could just picture Will Madison leering in at them. She squirmed uncomfortably, just thinking about it. Suppose Will called the police and reported they had broken in, or told their parents. Katie dropped the candy bars she was holding. Of course she wasn't going to eat them, she told herself. She was just looking at them.

"What shall we do, Sarah Lou?" she whispered.

"We could make funny noises and try to scare him away," Sarah Lou whispered.

"Will Madison?" Katie scoffed. "Scare him away! He'd be more likely to come and investigate. Let's just wait here quietly till he goes away," Katie suggested. She peeped out again. "He's still skipping stones."

"Shall we eat some candy while we wait?" Sarah Lou asked.

"No, Sarah Lou," Katie said, horrified. "That's stealing. Put them back."

"All right," Sarah Lou reluctantly agreed. "But I'm hungry."

The girls sat down on the dusty floor and took

turns checking on Will. When they heard him whistling again, Katie got up to look and ducked in a hurry.

"Get back," she whispered. "He's coming this way." The whistling came nearer and nearer until it sounded as though it was right outside the stand. They heard him rap on one of the windows, and they squeezed back under the counter as far as they could. It was very dusty, and Katie suddenly wanted to sneeze. She buried her face in her knees and held her nose.

Finally they heard the whistling get fainter. When at last there was silence, Sarah Lou looked out cautiously.

"There he goes across the field," she announced in a normal voice, and straightened up.

"Thank goodness," Katie sighed. "Hurry, let's get out of here before he looks around and sees us."

They climbed out of the stand, closed the window, and hurried off across the meadow in the opposite direction from Will. But when Katie looked back, Will was standing still, watching them.

"Sarah Lou," Katie panted, "I think he's looking at us."

"Well, he'll just have to look," Sarah Lou said, stopping for breath. "I have to slow down. Besides, Katie, there's nothing wrong with walking through a field."

"I know," Katie worried, "but do you think he saw us climb out of the stand?"

Will was walking off across the field again and Sarah Lou shrugged casually. "See, Katie, he's going away. I don't think he saw us. Anyway, what could he do about it?"

"He could get us into trouble, that's what." Katie frowned as she walked slowly behind Sarah Lou, thinking about it. It was scary, Katie thought, how you could get into trouble sometimes without even meaning to. And to think that this time she had been in the wrong and Will had been in the right!

The Ghost

Katie tried to stay out of Will's way the next day, so that he couldn't ask her any questions about what she had been doing at the refreshment stand. She waited till she saw him leave for school on his bike, and when she heard the Potters' dog bark she knew he had turned the corner. At school she and Sarah Lou managed to keep away from him on the playground.

"I just don't want him to ask us any questions," Katie told Sarah Lou. "What if he tells everybody at school about it? What if he tells our teacher?"

"He's such a big pest, anyway," Sarah Lou said. "But I don't think he saw us. Don't worry, Katie. I wish I could play with you again this afternoon, but I have to go to the dentist."

After school Katie went home by herself. As she came up Apple Street she saw Dick backing his car down the driveway. The car wouldn't go forward yet, so when he got out to the street he had to push it back up the driveway. Short Stuff and Will and Bob Potter were there.

"Hi, Katie," Will called out in a high silly voice, but she wouldn't answer him. She decided to water her garden, while she was trying to think of some things she could do by herself. She could always read, of course, or rearrange her doll collection, or maybe make some cookies. But it was such a nice sunny spring afternoon she didn't want to go in the house.

Katie turned off the hose, still undecided, and wandered across the yard. She climbed up on some logs stacked by the wall that enclosed Mr. Johnson's garden, and looked over at his house. She wondered again if she ought to write him about the ghost. Of course it wasn't a real ghost, she reminded herself, because there wasn't any such thing as a real ghost.

Katie's gaze moved over the garden — the rose bushes and the narrow little walks. Then she noticed a cluster of strawberry plants near the wall. They were thick with large ripe berries.

"Wait till you see what I'm going to get," she called out to Dick and the other boys as she crossed the driveway. But they were busy pushing the car and didn't even answer. Katie felt a little shiver of excitement as she went through the gate. The Johnson house was such a nice one

—white brick with wide green shutters. She tried not to think of the shutters. It wasn't possible that such a pretty house could be haunted. Wait till the girls heard she had gone back into the garden.

Katie hurried across the grass to the strawberry patch and began to pick the berries. The house remained quiet behind her and pretty soon she began to relax. After all, she was next to her own yard and she could hear the boy's voices.

Katie picked and ate and picked some more until the basket she had brought with her was almost full. Then it came. Crash! Katie spun around in horror. As she watched, the shutter opened and banged shut. Katie thought she saw something else, something that looked like an arm, a sleeve maybe. But when a white form appeared at the window Katie ran.

She raced across the garden, breathless with fright, and ran down the driveway. Just as she reached the front sidewalk she dropped the basket of berries. As she knelt to pick them up, she kept a wary eye on the house, ready to scream if she saw anything.

A minute later she heard the sound of a window closing. It was a little noise, and yet she was sure she had heard it. Katie jumped behind the shrubbery beside the driveway and crouched down so that she could peer through the bushes. Her heart thumped crazily. Then she caught a glimpse of a figure behind the bushes by the side of Mr. Johnson's house. She watched it straighten up and come toward her.

It was a boy — why, it was Will. Katie stared in astonishment. Will Madison! What was he doing there? Katie waited till Will had passed her, then she slipped around the bushes. When she was sure he had gone, she went back to the house. Her hands felt icy cold, but she had to find out what Will had been doing.

She looked behind the bushes at the side of the house. There, stuffed into the branches, was a piece of white cloth, and stuck into the ground was a wire coat hanger that had been bent out straight. Katie stared at them while her mind put it all together. The piece of cloth was the white "ghost" she had seen at the window. And the wire . . . Katie paused, thinking about it. Why, of course. The wire would push the shutter open and shut. The window would have to be opened only a crack to slip the wire through. No one in the garden would be able to see this. Yes, that was it. The end of the wire had been bent to make a hook. The image of the shutter opening and closing flashed through Katie's mind. But how did he get in the house? Katie tried the window and it slid up easily. Unlocked! This explained how Will got in.

Katie gathered up the cloth and wire. Now she'd really get that Will Madison in trouble, and that was just what he deserved. He had no right scaring her friends and keeping them from coming over.

But a better idea suddenly occurred to Katie as she stood in the driveway. She could hear Dick's car backing out, and she quickly dashed back and hid the cloth and wire where she'd found them. She'd show that Will Madison this time, really show him.

On the way back home she stopped to watch the boys as they pushed the car back up the driveway once again. Will was with them, looking as innocent as could be.

"Look at the strawberries I picked over in Mr. Johnson's yard," Katie called gaily. She waved the basket toward them. She thought Will looked at her strangely, but the others didn't pay any attention.

"Here," she went on as the car stopped, "would you like some?" Katie thrust the basket in through the window.

"Thanks, Katie," Short Stuff said, grabbing a handful.

"I thought you were scared to go over there," Dick said, helping himself to the strawberries.

"Oh, it's not that bad," Katie replied, looking straight at Will. She could hardly keep from laughing. "When I thought I saw a ghost this afternoon, I just ran off. Have some strawberries, Will?" she said politely.

She could afford to be nice to Will, considering what she had in store for him.

The Ghost Party

Katie had a terrible time that evening keeping quiet about what she had discovered. She longed to tell someone, most of all Sarah Lou. But she didn't dare telephone her for fear someone in the living room would overhear the conversation. Besides, if Sarah Lou knew, she'd tell Jody, then Jody would tell someone, and it wouldn't be a secret anymore. She couldn't tell Dick; he would probably feel he had to say something to Will. And if she told Jamie, he'd be sure to blab. He wouldn't mean to, of course, but he never could keep a secret.

So Katie bided her time and made her plans. She asked Dick if he would be working on his car the next afternoon. He said, yes, indeed, that soon he would have it running in all directions. "I didn't know you were interested in my car," he asked, looking up from his homework. "Why do you want to know?"

"Oh, just wondering," Katie said casually. It

would help her plans if Dick worked on his car tomorrow. It was important that the boys be there when she did what she was going to do. She'd better be careful, though, or Dick would know she was up to something. But maybe after tomorrow Dick wouldn't take Will's side all the time.

At school the next day Katie told her friends that she was going to have a little party at her house that afternoon, and if they'd come over after school she'd have a surprise for them. Jody and Sarah Lou, Mary and Sue kept asking her what it was, but Katie wouldn't tell. She knew it would be all over school in no time if she did, and then she couldn't play her trick on Will.

Just to make sure that Will would be there, Katie wrote a note and slipped it into his desk during the noon recess. In big block letters she printed: "Will, please come to Mr. Johnson's backyard at four this afternoon. There will be something there for you." She signed it with a big X.

During the first period after lunch — it was Miss Pratt's English class — she saw Will find the note. He read it a couple of times, then he looked around at the class, suspiciously. Katie quickly looked down at her book. A minute later out of the corner of her eye she saw Will toss the note back in his desk.

Would he come? Yes, Katie reassured herself. Will was much too curious to pass up something like this.

After school Katie brought all the girls home with her. "We're going to have the surprise at four o'clock," she promised them, "over in Mr. Johnson's yard."

"Not over there!" exclaimed Sarah Lou.

"It's safe, I promise," Katie said.

"But how do you know?" Sarah Lou insisted.

"I found out what the ghost is," Katie answered, revealing part of her secret. "And believe me, it's safe."

The girls begged her to tell them more, but Katie only smiled and shook her head.

"You have to come with me to find out," she said.

Her friends protested, but they finally agreed to come. They walked up Mr. Johnson's driveway, holding hands and giggling nervously. Katie ran ahead.

"I'm going in here," she said, pointing to the window at the side of the house. "All of you hide behind the bushes in the garden and be quiet. The ghost is coming."

"Oh, Katie," moaned Sarah Lou.

"Are you sure you know what you're doing?" Jody asked.

"Yes, yes," Katie assured them. "You'll see. Go

hide now," she commanded, "and don't give me away."

She collected the piece of cloth and the wire and eased open the window. This was the only part she didn't like, going into the empty house alone. She had to remind herself that Will was the only ghost. She had been in Mr. Johnson's house before, so she knew where all the rooms were. She climbed the winding stairs to the top floor and walked down the long hall. Without any furniture in the house the rooms seemed twice as large, and her footsteps echoed loudly on the wooden floors.

Katie shivered and hurried to the back bedroom windows overlooking the garden. There was no sign of Will or the girls; the garden looked deserted. Then, as if in answer to her wish, she saw Will hoist himself up on the wall. He sat there, straddling it for a minute and staring all around. He looked puzzled. Then he jumped down and walked quickly toward the summerhouse. Katie hoped the girls wouldn't make any noise.

Carefully she pushed the window up a tiny bit, stuck the wire hanger through it, and hooked it onto the shutter. Then, staying out of sight, she pushed the shutter open, then pulled it shut with a bang. Will spun around to stare at the window. Katie did it again, laughing to herself, and then she waved the white cloth in front of the window.

"Heyyy," she heard Will yell. Katie threw open the window and leaned out.

"Hi, Will," she called.

The girls burst out from behind the bushes.

Will looked as if he'd like to hide forever. Katie waved the cloth at him, then closed the window. She gathered up the wire and the cloth and ran downstairs.

By the time she got out to the garden, Dick, Bob Potter, and Short Stuff had come over and were asking the girls what was going on. Will tried to look innocent, but he seemed nervous.

"Katie, what's this all about?" demanded Dick.

"Katie, you were doing that, weren't you?" Sarah Lou giggled. Will didn't say anything at all. He just looked more and more uncomfortable.

"Here, Will Madison," Katie said, handing him the cloth and the wire. "Here are your ghost things. Thanks for letting me use them."

"Why, Katie, but . . . but. . ." Will sputtered. For once he didn't seem able to talk.

"Here, take them," Katie insisted. "You had so much fun with them. Wouldn't you like to scare some more people?"

"Aw, Katie," Will said. His face turned bright red and he tried to laugh. He really looked miserable now. "I didn't mean to, really. It was just supposed to be a joke."

"Will Madison! You might know," Jody said.

Then Jamie, who had come running into the garden spoke up. "Will, were you really the ghost?" he asked, wide-eyed. "Gollllly." Will looked more uncomfortable than ever.

"I only meant to scare the girls a little, that's all," Will said to the boys.

Bob and Dick just stood there, half-grinning and staring at Will. They didn't seem to know quite what to say either. Then Short Stuff stepped up to Katie and said, "Will told me about being the ghost, Katie, but he didn't mean any real harm."

"Not much," Katie sniffed. "You see, we didn't imagine it," she said, turning to Dick.

"I guess not," Dick conceded. "I'll have to admit you did see something. But it was only old Will, not a ghost after all."

"Yes, but who knew that?" Katie retorted. "It was a dumb thing to do, you'll have to admit."

Katie stalked off, taking the girls back to her house, where they had cookies and milk and talked about what an awful pest Will Madison was.

After her friends left, Katie decided to write Mr. Johnson a letter. She had the little white business card he had given her tucked away in her desk drawer. First she told him that she missed him and wondered if he was still trying to sell his house because there weren't any people

47

coming to look at it. Then she told him Dick mowed the lawn and they both helped weed the flower beds. She said she loved playing in the summerhouse, and she had done another good thing — she had rid the house of ghosts. It was a long letter by the time she finished up with a vivid description of Will as the ghost. In a postscript she wrote that she hoped someone with a girl would buy the house as it was difficult being the only girl on Apple Street.

Katie stamped the letter and took it down to the mailbox at the corner by the Potters' house. She hoped she would get an answer soon.

Rescued

Will was teased at school. The girls all called him "Ghostie," and even some of the boys joined in. The teasing lasted right up to the end of school. Katie almost felt sorry for him a couple of times, until she remembered that her friends never wanted to play in Mr. Johnson's yard anymore. Somehow the spell had been broken and the fun had gone out of it, even though they knew there was no ghost.

They said there were too many boys at Katie's house anyway, and why not play at Sarah Lou's or Sue's or Jody's. When they wanted to play in the front yard at Katie's house, the boys would start a game. In the back, they worked on the car, and up in Katie's room Jamie and Bobby would come and pester them.

Dick kept on mowing Mr. Johnson's lawn, but there was still no answer from him. Mrs. Hart was getting worried. And it had been weeks now since Katie had written.

Summer vacation finally arrived, with long cool evenings and bright hot days. It was delicious to wake up in the morning and have nothing to do.

One morning in early summer when Katie awoke, she lay in bed wriggling her toes and watching the sunlight fall in slanting streaks across her room. She could hear a lawn mower whirring somewhere, and the birds singing in the trees beside her window. It felt like a special day, a day to go to the woods, to go on a picnic. Katie jumped out of bed and hurried to call Sarah Lou.

Luckily, Jody was away visiting her grand-mother, so Sarah Lou agreed to go. After break-fast the girls set out for the woods, dressed in jeans, knitted shirts, and sneakers. The sun was warming up as they hurried across the little bridge over the creek. Inside the patch of woods that stretched along the far side of the creek it was cool and the sounds of Apple Street were far off. Dry leaves crunched under their feet, and once in a while a rabbit hopped away in the bushes. They followed a footpath that wound in and out among the trees.

"Let's go through here," Katie suggested, pointing to a thick stand of trees farther back from the creek. "We'll make our own path."

They pushed their way through the bushes, stopping to feel the soft green moss that grew on the north side of the trees. They picked some red currant berries and squeezed the juice all over their fingers.

"We could paint our faces with this," Sarah Lou giggled.

"Look, there's a bigger bush over there." Katie squeezed through heavy undergrowth to get to it. "Sarah Lou! Oh, come here," Katie called excitedly. Katie pointed to a big patch of green moss on the ground completely encircled by bushes.

"Oh, what a wonderful hideaway." Sarah Lou sighed with delight. "Let's go in," she urged.

The girls got down on their knees, crawled through the scratchy bushes, and stretched out on the soft green carpet of moss. It was cool and quiet and far away from everything. They lay on their backs, gazing up at the fluttering leaves overhead. Outside was a sunny golden world: Within their little circle it was submerged and green, like being underwater.

After a few minutes Sarah Lou sat up. "I'm hungry," she announced. "Let's eat lunch here."

They ate quietly, hushed by the woods. When they had finished they picked up the sandwich papers and even brushed the crumbs off the moss. As they were about to leave their cool green world, there was a sudden rustling in the bushes around them.

"What was that?" Sarah Lou stared at Katie, but before Katie could answer the bushes shook again.

Katie clutched Sarah Lou's arm. "Shhhh, listen."

All at once their cool green world seemed too far away from Apple Street. In fact, it seemed frightening.

"Quick, let's get out of here," Sarah Lou whispered, backing away.

Then there came a strange, low moaning. Katie and Sarah Lou didn't wait any longer. They tore through the scratchy bushes and raced for the creek. To their embarrassment they heard shouts of laughter behind them. Turning, they saw Will and Short Stuff bent double with laughter.

"Whoooo," the boys moaned.

"Oh, for goodness sakes!" exclaimed Katie, disgustedly. "What a pest. That Will Madison, he will never change."

"You might know," Sarah Lou said as she looked at the boys crossly. "Now they've found our hideaway. You know, Katie, whenever I play with you we always get mixed up with those boys. Jody and I never have any trouble."

"Well you don't live in a neighborhood full of boys," Katie sighed. "Let's go down to the lake. We'll just ignore them." That Will, she thought hopelessly, he'll just go on trying to scare me and tease me forever.

But Will and Short Stuff had apparently lost interest in the girls; they didn't follow them any farther. When Sarah Lou and Katie reached the lake, they decided to go wading. They took off their sneakers and walked along the edge of the lake. The mud squished through their toes, and the water that lapped at their ankles felt cold and fresh.

Walking on ahead of Sarah Lou, Katie made a discovery: Pulled up on the shore and partly hidden in the tall grass was an old gray rowboat. When she pushed the boat on its side, she saw the oars stored under the seats.

"Look, look what I've found," she called.

Sarah Lou came running up to her.

"How wonderful!" marveled Sarah Lou. Her eyes sparkled. "Let's go for a row."

"Wouldn't it be fun?" Katie agreed. "Do you think anybody'd mind?"

"We'll bring it right back," Sarah Lou said. "We'll just go for a little boat ride."

It was quite a job to push the old rowboat into the water, but they finally eased it off the muddy shore. It was shallow near the edge of the lake, and they could wade out into the water before climbing into the boat.

"Oh, what fun," Katie shouted. "Here, Sarah Lou, sit beside me. Let's row."

Each of the girls handled an oar, and they paddled slowly around, turning clumsily in circles. "Come on, Sarah Lou, let's try to row *together*." Katie laughed.

The boys were completely forgotten now and nowhere to be seen. After a little practice the girls got the boat going more smoothly and almost before they knew it they were quite far out from shore. The old boat bobbed lazily on the water and the sun felt warm on their backs. Then suddenly Katie noticed that water was seeping into the boat.

"Sarah Lou!" she exclaimed, "the boat's leaking!" The girls stared anxiously at the bottom of the boat as the water continued to rise.

"Oh, Katie," Sarah Lou said nervously. "It's really pouring in now. Let's go back."

"I'll row and you bail," Katie said, grabbing the oars. Sarah Lou started scooping the water out with her two hands. Katie bent over the oars, trying to row as fast as she could. Sarah Lou scooped wildly. But the water was really pouring in now and rising higher and higher inside the boat.

"Oh, it's hopeless," Sarah Lou groaned. "Here, I'll try to row with you instead."

But the old boat, heavy with water, would hardly move in spite of their efforts.

"What shall we do?" Sarah Lou looked frightened as she paused to rest her arms. "I'm getting tired from rowing."

"It's a long way to shore," Katie pointed out. "Think we could swim?"

"It's pretty far," Sarah Lou said, doubtfully. "I've had swimming lessons but I don't know if I could swim *that* far." Katie saw the frightened look in Sarah Lou's eyes and she grew more worried.

"We could just stay here and hang onto the boat," Katie suggested. "It probably won't go very far under. I saw Dick try to sink a rowboat one time, and it just floated around a few inches under the water."

"It would get pretty cold," Sarah Lou responded with a shiver.

They sat with their feet tucked under them, to keep them out of the water, and wondered what to do. Katie looked again at the shore, and then at the water rising in the boat. The refreshment stand and the dock seemed very far away, but there were a few people moving about. If she only could make them hear or see.

"Help, heeeelp!" Katie cupped her mouth and screamed toward shore, but no one appeared to hear. Sarah Lou joined in, but still nothing happened. The water was almost up to the seats now.

"We'll stay here in the boat as long as we can," Katie said firmly, "and then we'll just have to swim." Katie wasn't worried for herself. She knew she could make it, although she didn't like the idea of swimming such a long way in deep water. But it was Sarah Lou she was worried about. "If we float on our backs and rest a lot we can make it, I know," she assured her friend.

"I guess so," Sarah Lou agreed, but she looked frightened.

Katie tried to think of some way she could help Sarah Lou when they were in the water. "Maybe you could rest your hand on my shoulder from time to time," she suggested.

"Or I could start dog-paddling when I get tired," Sarah Lou said hopefully. "I always seem to go under when I float." She began to shiver again.

Just then a loud shout came from the shore and there, suddenly, was Will Madison, standing at the water's edge.

"Heyyyy!" he shouted.

"Oh, there's Will," Sarah Lou said with a gasp of relief. "Do you suppose he could help?"

Will wasn't laughing or teasing this time. He was waving his arms and shouting.

"Maybe he could bring help!" Katie exclaimed.

She jumped up, rocking the heavy boat, and waved back. "Help, we're sinking!" she shouted.

It was a needless thing to say because the old boat was so low in the water now it was quite obvious that they were sinking.

"Hold on," Will shouted and then ran along the shore, looking through the tall grass as though he were searching for something. Before long he found what he wanted: He dragged an old log down to the shore, shoved it into the water, and dove in after it.

"Look," Sarah Lou cried excitedly. "He's coming."

"Hurray!" shouted Katie, clapping her hands. She stood up in the boat and cupped her mouth again. "Come on, come on," she called joyfully. "Isn't this wonderful, Sarah Lou?" she shouted. Sarah Lou was laughing shakily, and Katie suddenly realized that her friend might not have made the long swim to shore. It was a frightening thought.

Will was coming rapidly toward them, pushing the log along in front of him by kicking his feet. Before he reached them, the water had risen over the seats in the boat. Katie and Sarah Lou stood up shakily on the seats, ready to slip into the water. When Will reached the boat, the girls went over the side and hung onto the log.

"I thought I better rescue you myself instead

of wasting time going for help," Will said, shaking the water out of his hair. "I was over there fishing when I heard you."

"Oh, thank you, Will," Katie said, clutching the log. "Sarah Lou wasn't sure she could make it."

"It's okay," Will said. He looked embarrassed.

"I was scared," Sarah Lou confessed, resting her chin on the log. "And I sure thank you, Will. It looked such an awful long way."

"That'll teach you to go out in some beat-up old boat," Will grinned. "And don't forget to report what happened to the boat."

"Oh yes, I will." Katie was conscience-stricken. She knew they should never have taken the boat.

"Well, let's go," Will said, blowing bubbles in the water. Katie was grateful to him for not saying any more about the boat. "I won't tell on you this time either," he added suddenly, lifting his face out of the water and looking at her seriously.

"Why, what do you mean?" Katie gasped.

"I saw you over there that day." Will nodded toward the refreshment stand and grinned knowingly. "And I didn't get you into trouble that time either. You hang onto the log," he added, "and I'll swim alongside."

"What does he mean, Katie? Sarah Lou whispered.

"I guess he did see us that day," Katie said slowly.

"And he didn't even tell on us! You know something, Katie I guess he isn't so bad after all."

Katie had to agree. In fact, she thought about Will all the way in to shore as she and Sarah Lou kicked and paddled behind the log. Will had certainly been nice, there was no doubt about that. And who would have thought she would ever be thinking a thing like that about Will Madison?

Letters

Hot midsummer days arrived, and still nothing happened with Mr. Johnson's house. Most afternoons Katie and Jamie went down to the creek to go swimming. Usually some of Katie's friends from school were there too. They swam and ate ice cream and sat on the edge of the dock in the sun. Although the afternoons were fun, the evenings were lonely. All the boys went off to play together, and Katie wandered around alone. As it turned dark the boys came home and sometimes they played hide-and-seek. Then Katie joined them.

One afternoon when she and Jamie came home from swimming, her mother met them at the door.

"I knew you wouldn't want me to open this," her mother said, handing Katie a long white envelope. "It's from Redingford."

"Mr. Johnson!" Katie exclaimed excitedly as she tore the envelope open. He had written a long letter in very small handwriting, which was rather difficult to read. Katie and her mother read the letter together.

Mr. Johnson thanked Katie for writing and thanked Dick for looking after his property. Then he went on to explain that he had taken his house off the market after the Walters agreed to buy it. Then just when Mr. Walters had been transferred out West and the family couldn't take the house, he had to go into the hospital unexpectedly. He'd been in the hospital for quite a while, but now he was back in his apartment and he was going to try to sell the house again. He said he needed to sell it quickly. He thanked Katie for her long report and said it was the best letter he'd ever received and that he would read it many times. At the end he said he liked living in Redingford very much; his daughter visited him every day and he had some nice friends in his apartment building. In a postscript he added that he sympathized with Katie, having to live in a neighborhood of only boys, although he didn't see what he could do about it.

"Poor Mr. Johnson," Mrs. Hart said when they'd finished. "Here he's been having a difficult time and none of us even knew about it. It's a lovely letter he's written you, dear."

"I'm glad he's better now," Katie said, thinking it must not be fun to be sick. She wished she could help him sell his house.

When she showed the letter to Dick he said scornfully, "What's the use of telling him you'd like a girl next door? Mr. Johnson has to sell his house to the first buyer who comes along. He needs the money. You can't expect him to turn down a good offer just because they don't have a girl in the family, can you?"

"No, of course not," Katie answered, taking the letter back from Dick. "I just thought I'd mention it, that's all."

"And why did you have to tell him about Will? He saved you and Sarah Lou the day you went out in that boat."

"Well, it's Mr. Johnson's house," Katie defended herself. "Will had no right going in there."

"I know. But he didn't hurt anything," Dick said.

"You always stand up for him," Katie replied, almost in tears. "You boys always stick together. Will scared all my friends away. You don't care about that. Your friends are here all the time." Katie began to feel cross.

"Now Katie, don't get angry." Dick grinned. "When your friends get a little older, they'll like to come over here where there are so many boys."

"Never," Katie said, thinking that was surely the most ridiculous thing she'd ever heard. "They don't like boys."

Dick burst out laughing and grabbed Katie and tickled her until she squealed for mercy.

"Would you play cards with me now?" she asked, once she had got free of him.

"No, I have to work on my car," Dick said, starting for the door. It seemed to Katie that he never had any time for her since he'd gotten that car. "Who knows?" he called over his shoulder. "Maybe someday I'll give you a ride in it."

Katie thought and thought about Mr. Johnson's letter. If only she could help him sell his house, but to people with a girl of course. Katie went to bed that night thinking about it. Her father always said it was best to sleep on a problem, and that was just what she would do.

It worked too, because in the morning Katie woke with an idea. No sooner were her eyes open than the idea flew into her mind. She lay still thinking it over for a minute, and then she jumped out of bed. She hurried to her desk and took out her best stationery and started to write a letter to the local newspaper.

First she wrote about Mr. Johnson's disappointment when the buyers had to move out West, and then she explained that he had been in the hospital. Now the house was a burden to him, she wrote, and he really needed to sell it. She went on to describe her neighborhood, all the boys, and her brothers, the ball games on the front lawn, the old car, and even Wilbur, the toad. But it was lonesome being surrounded by so many boys, she wrote. She ended the letter with the wish that the newspaper could help find a family with a girl, who might buy the house.

Katie decided to mail the letter without telling anyone. They'd only laugh at her, and she knew it was a silly thing to do anyway. Still in her pajamas, she went downstairs to get a stamp from her father's desk and copy the address off the newspaper.

After breakfast Katie rode her bike to the mailbox in front of the Potters' house and dropped in her letter. But no sooner had she mailed it than she wished she hadn't. If only she could reach in and take it back. How silly it was. Her face burned at the thought of people reading it. What would her mother and father say. What would Dick say! Katie wished again that she had never written the letter.

As she returned home, she saw Jamie crawling among the bushes in front of the house.

"What are you doing?" Katie asked, puzzled. "Trying to hide from Bobby or something?"

"No," came Jamie's voice from the bushes. "I'm looking for Wilbur." Jamie talked as though his mouth were full of leaves.

"What did you bring him out for?" Katie asked. "He could get away."

"He did get away," Jamie spoke sadly. "But

Wilbur likes to get out once in a while." Jamie's worried face showed between the bushes. "Wilbur likes the sunshine and the fresh air too, you know."

Katie wanted to go over to Sarah Lou's house to tell her about the letter, but Jamie looked so upset she couldn't leave him.

"You like to go outside too, don't you?" Jamie asked defiantly.

"Of course," Katie said impatiently. "But I'm not a toad and I won't hop away."

"It's not funny," Jamie's voice came from the bushes, which began to shake again.

"I'll help you," Katie said, dropping to her knees, "but I don't know how we'll ever find him." Katie took one side of the bushes and Jamie the other and together they searched around among the old dead leaves.

"Wilbur! Wilbur!" Jamie called, even though he knew it was no use calling a toad.

"Have you two gone nutty?" a voice suddenly spoke above them.

"We're looking for Wilbur," Katie explained, as she looked up at Will, a little embarrassed that he should come along just then.

"You mean he got away?" Will said seriously. "Say, Jamie, that's too bad. How long has he been out here?"

"Not very long," Jamie spoke from his end of the bushes.

"Maybe he's still around then," Will said. "Here, I'll help you look." At times Will could be very helpful, Katie had to admit.

Suddenly Will gave a tremendous shout and a jump. "I got him!" he said grinning. "Quick, Jamie, let's put him in the box."

"Thanks a lot, Will," Jamie shouted happily, rushing forward. "Wilbur's probably glad too," he said, tucking the toad back in his box. "Anytime you want to, you can hold Wilbur."

"Thanks." Will grinned. "But I got to go now."

After Will left, Katie got back on her bike and set off for Sarah Lou's. As she pedaled she found herself thinking how nice Will had been lately, finding Wilbur for Jamie, and helping them the day she and Sarah Lou almost sank in the boat, and never telling about seeing them climb out of the refreshment stand. When she tried to thank him for that, he'd just said, "Oh, it was nothing." Maybe he was sorry for the things he'd done, for scaring her friends away and for tearing up her garden.

Now that Mr. Johnson's house was up for sale again, maybe — just maybe — her troubles were coming to an end. There was a chance. Maybe her letter to the paper would even do some good.

The Potters' Dog

When Katie returned home late that afternoon, she hurried around to the back to water her garden. It had been a very warm day and the vegetables would be dry. Jamie came out the back door to ask if he might help with the watering, and just as they were turning the corner of the garage, the Potters' red setter went tearing past and almost knocked them down.

"Oh," Katie gasped, "what's he doing back here?"

"He got out of his yard again," Jamie said behind her, but Katie was staring at her garden.

"Look what he's done!" she exclaimed. There were big holes dug in the garden, tomato plants ripped down, and other plants trampled. It wasn't as bad as the first time, but it was bad enough. It looked like the same kind of a job.

"That dog!" Katie burst out. "He's the one that did it. Why, that awful dog!"

"Boy, he really tore it up, didn't he?" Jamie

exclaimed beside her. "And he's still just a pup. I never knew a dog would dig up like that."

"I never did either," Katie said, almost tearfully. "Oh, my poor garden." She went down on her knees to gather up the carrots and tomatoes that lay strewn about.

"They look about big enough to eat now anyway," Jamie consoled her.

"I suppose they are," Katie said sadly, patting down the loose earth around the smaller plants and gathering up the ripened vegetables.

"We could eat them tonight," Jamie said. "They sure look good."

"Oh, Jamie!" she exclaimed suddenly, a stricken look on her face. "I thought Will did it. Oh, dear." Her father's words floated back to her: "You shouldn't accuse anyone of wrongdoing unless you have some proof."

And what proof had she had? None at all. She had just wildly accused Will. And why? Just because he seemed a likely one to have done it, and well, maybe because he had helped her and Sarah Lou swim in from the rowboat and of the way he'd helped Jamie find his toad. Of course he *had* thrown dirt on her garden at the very start. And he *had* scared the girls away with that silly ghost stuff and moved the "For Sale" sign, but still . . . all that wasn't very bad, really. And he hadn't told on her, even though she'd told on him once, in school.

Katie stood up slowly. Her face was burning with shame. She'd have to apologize to Will. Jamie was still gathering up bits of broken carrots.

"Jamie, will you come with me?" Katie asked.

"Sure," Jamie said loyally. "Where are we going?"

"To Will's to tell him about the dog," Katie said. "I have to apologize."

"What for?" Jamie asked curiously.

"I have to tell him I'm sorry," Katie said solemnly. "It's not going to be easy, but I have to do it . . . after the way I accused him."

"Aw, you were just mad at him. I could tell," Jamie said. Katie looked quickly at her little brother. Jamie was surprisingly shrewd at times.

"Well, anyway, I must do it," Katie said resolutely. "But please come with me, Jamie," she added.

She and Jamie dumped the vegetables in the kitchen sink and then walked over to Will's house. Katie suddenly wished she could run the other way, but she couldn't very well back out now — not with Jamie walking beside her. She knocked lightly on the Madisons' front door, hoping that somehow Will wouldn't be home and that she could talk to his mother instead. Mrs. Madison was a very understanding woman.

But when the door opened, there was Will. He

was in his baseball uniform and he looked surprised to see them.

"Don't tell me you lost Wilbur again," he said.

Jamie just shook his head.

Will looked at Katie, then grinned. The freckles sort of danced across his face. Katie noticed that his eyes matched the blue in his baseball cap.

"Something the matter with you, Goody Two-Shoes?" he asked.

"Uh, well," Katie forced herself to stand there. His joking didn't make things any easier. She knew she was blushing.

"What's the matter with her?" Will asked Jamie.

"She's got something important to tell you," Jamie said gravely. "It's about her garden. Go on, Katie," he said, giving her a nudge.

"Oh, Will, I'm so sorry," Katie burst out all in a rush. "I just found out . . . it was Bob Potter's dog that dug up my garden . . . he did it again just now . . . and it wasn't you at all. . . ."

"Why, I knew it was Red all along," Will grinned. "He's only a pup, you know."

"Well, I'm sorry, Will, honest I am," Katie said nervously, wishing she were back home. "I should never accuse people without good reason."

Will was beginning to look a little embarrassed too. "Aw, forget about it, Katie. Listen, I got to get to the ball game. I can't stand here gabbing all day. So long, Jamie," and he shut the door abruptly.

Katie sighed with relief and turned to go. Thank goodness that was over. At dinner that evening she told her family the whole story. Dick said he hoped she'd learned a lesson, and her mother said she hoped Katie was sorry for having talked that way about Will, but that she had done the right thing to apologize.

Her father said, "Remember, Katie, a man's innocent until he's proven guilty. Don't go around saying things about people unless you know they're true."

Katie nodded sadly. She knew she hadn't been fair. She remembered that she had told all her friends at school that Will had torn up her garden. The phone rang just then interrupting her thoughts. Jamie ran to answer it.

"Dick," he called from the hall. "It's for you. It's a girl," he added in a loud voice. Dick looked embarrassed as he got up from the table.

Katie saw her mother smile at her father and she sensed that something had been going on that she hadn't been aware of. Dick had a girl friend — Dick, who had never been interested in girls. Katie couldn't believe it, but then she realized that Dick had been making a lot of phone calls lately and he spent more time getting dressed in the mornings.

"Dick's gotta girl," Jamie sang out when Dick returned to the table.

"You talk too much, Jamie," Dick muttered.

"Guess what I found Dick doing the other morning," Jamie went on in a loud voice.

Mrs. Hart looked at him and said in a warning voice, "Jamie."

But Katie couldn't resist asking.

"He was shaving," Jamie told her.

"Shaving!" Katie said in amazement, and stared at her big brother. "Is he old enough?"

"Well, what if I was?" Dick said.

"And he cut himself in two places," Jamie continued. "There was blood dripping all over the place."

Katie remembered the morning Dick had come down with Band-Aids on his face. When she had asked him what happened he had just said it was nothing, just a couple of little mosquito bites.

"Jamie, why don't you keep quiet?" Dick said crossly.

Mr. Hart picked up the evening paper and hid behind it.

"And he's always fixing his hair," Jamie went on. "And — "

"Jamie, that will do now," Mrs. Hart said firmly.

Later, as they were playing catch on the front lawn, Katie was relieved that she hadn't told Jamie about her letter to the paper. She wouldn't want him teasing her the way he had just teased Dick. But how she wished she could help Mr. Johnson sell his house, and how she hoped some nice girl would move there.

"Katie," Jamie said, breaking in on her thoughts. "You know, all those phone calls and all that stuff about Dick lately?"

"Yes," Katie said, "what about it?"

"I know Dick's got a girl." Jamie paused long enough for Katie to be impressed. "Do you think some day you'll be getting phone calls from Will Madison?"

"How silly," Katie said crossly. "You know I don't like him. Except for now and then," she added fairly, remembering how nice he'd been about her apology that afternoon.

"I bet you will," Jamie grinned. "In fact, I think he likes you already. I can tell 'cause he's always picking on you."

Katie was so dumbfounded by this remark that she missed the ball Jamie threw to her and had to run way down the street to get it. What a ridiculous idea. If she was ever going to be anybody's girl, it certainly wouldn't be Will Madison's. No sir, it'd be some boy who didn't tease her and play tricks on her.

And then Katie wondered, for a moment, what Will's voice would sound like on the telephone.

Prospective Buyers

Katie fell asleep that night thinking about Dick and Will and Bob Potter's dog and her letter to the paper. When she woke in the morning she distinctly remembered having a dream in which she'd seen a picture of Bob Potter's dog on the front page of the local newspaper. The caption underneath the picture said, "New owner of house on Apple Street."

Katie laughed and wondered about her letter. The editor probably threw it away, she told herself. He must get hundreds of letters all the time.

Katie was still thinking about her letter a few minutes later when she sat down to a delicious breakfast of waffles. She smothered them with butter and syrup and was taking the first delicious bite when she heard her father mutter.

"What's this?" He spoke drom the depths of his newspaper. Katie took another bite, not paying any attention. "What is this?" her father repeated, lowering the paper.

"What is what, dear?" Mrs. Hart asked, looking out over her half of the paper.

"Listen to this letter to the editor," Mr. Hart said. He cleared his throat as he started to read.

" 'Dear Editor: We have quite a problem in our neighborhood and I wonder if you could help us. One of our neighbors has moved to an apartment in another town. He has been sick, and he needs to sell his house. My mother says it was just too much for him to keep up. Someone is bound to buy it, but I'm hoping someone with girls, not boys.' "

Katie had stopped eating and was staring at her father. She tingled all over as she heard her words being read aloud.

" 'We have so many boys in our neighborhood,' " her father continued, with an amazed look on his face. Mrs. Hart fastened her eyes on him. " 'There are my brothers, Dick and Jamie; Will next door and his friend Short Stuff; Jamie's friend Bobby; Bob Potter and his big dog, Red; and some others. But I am the only girl. We also have a toad called Wilbur because he's probably a boy toad also. It's a good neighborhood for boys, and girls too. Next door to us,' " Mr. Hart read on, and his voice sounded even more surprised, " 'is the vacant house which the owner needs to sell. He's a very nice man and he's been having a hard time lately. His house has a pretty garden in the back with a summerhouse. I think it would be nice if a girl moved in there. Is there anything you can do?' ''

Katie put down her fork. She couldn't listen any longer. She felt embarrassed and happy at the same time. They had printed her letter! She was much too excited to finish her waffles. Would people really read it, and what would they think?

"Katie," her father spoke to her gently, "Did you write this letter?"

Katie nodded, suddenly worried that her parents would be angry. But no, her father was looking at her with a kind of surprised smile on his face.

"You mean Katie wrote that?" Dick exclaimed. He looked at Katie with amazement. "Not bad, Katie, not bad at all. But you needn't sound so miserable just because there are a lot of boys around here."

"Why, Katie." Her mother beamed proudly. "What a nice letter, and just to think they printed it. Won't Mr. Johnson be pleased."

"Katie's in the newspaper!" exclaimed Jamie as the truth came to him. "Just like the President."

"Not quite," Dick grinned.

"I just can't get over it," marveled Mrs. Hart. "Poor girl, you would like a little playmate close by."

Katie sighed. Her mother always referred to

her friends as little playmates. Probably even when she was in junior high her mother would call her friends little playmates.

"But what good will that letter do?" Dick pointed out practically. Katie wondered about that too.

"Well, maybe none," Mr. Hart answered, "but you never can tell." He shook his head, smiling. "Who would have thought it? Our Katie. But you have lots of friends, Katie — Sarah Lou and Jody and — "

"Oh yes, school friends," Katie interrupted. "But it's so far to their houses, even on my bike, and they all live close together. Mostly they don't want to come way out here unless something special comes up."

The telephone rang and Dick went to answer it. It was Nona Mitchell, one of Mrs. Hart's best friends.

"Nona's probably seen the paper," Mrs. Hart said. And a moment later Katie heard her mother saying, "Yes, indeed, that was our Katie. Yes, really." There was a long pause and then Mrs. Hart said, "Yes, isn't it exciting? Thank you, Nona. Poor child, she does need a playmate."

In a moment Mrs. Hart came back, smiling. "Well, Katie, Mrs. Mitchell was so impressed with your letter and she . . . "

The telephone rang again and Mrs. Hart went

back to answer it. Katie heard her mother laugh and then say, "Yes, indeed, that was our Katie. Yes, she really did write it."

"Oh, not again," groaned Dick. "All this publicity. I hope it does some good."

"It might help sell the house, mightn't it, Dad?" Katie appealed to Mr. Hart. "Even if the *Telegram* isn't a very big paper."

"It might," Mr. Hart said. "But I wouldn't count on it, Katie."

Once again Mrs. Hart returned to the breakfast table. "That was Mrs. Madison," she explained. Katie wondered in a flash of embarrassment what Will would say about the letter.

The Harts had just barely finished breakfast when the telephone rang again.

"I don't know whether we can stand all this excitement," Mr. Hart said. "But if your mother has to keep answering the telephone, you better do the dishes, Katie."

Katie could hear her mother on the telephone, saying again, "Yes, yes, that was our Katie."

Katie was halfway through the dishes when the telephone rang again. This time it was Sarah Lou.

"Katie!" she shrieked. "Was that your letter?"

"Yes, it was." Katie smiled into the receiver as she heard the excitement in her friend's voice.

"Wait till Miss Pratt sees that," Sarah Lou went on. "Why, it was wonderful!"

Katie smiled again. It was nice to be praised.

"I never dreamed they'd print it," she said modestly.

"But listen, Katie, next time you get tired of all those boys you come right over to my house — anytime. My mother read your letter and said to be sure to tell you you could visit us anytime at all."

That was nice of Sarah Lou's mother, but *she* didn't understand either. It was fun to go visiting, but Katie didn't want to have to visit all the time. Although Sarah Lou was one of her very best friends, still, she and Jody seemed to have a secret understanding. Katie wished she had a special friend of her own too. Sarah Lou probably didn't realize how Katie felt either.

Later in the day the broker at the real estate office called.

"Such a charming letter," she told Katie's mother. "And do you know, we've received a number of calls from people who read it and want to see the house."

During the afternoon Katie thought she'd go over to Sarah Lou's, but when she saw a car pull up in front of Mr. Johnson's house she decided to stay home. Katie sat on the front steps, watching the house. In the backyard Dick and Bob Potter were working on the car. Katie could hear them racing the engine.

She decided to call Sarah Lou and ask if she wanted to come over and watch the people coming to see the house. Sarah Lou said that she and Jody were playing a really special game, and couldn't Katie come over there. Katie said she couldn't and wished silently that Sarah Lou and Jody weren't always playing some special game.

After she hung up the phone, Katie went out to the backyard to watch the boys. Jamie and his friend Bobby were sitting on the grass watching the bigger boys. The car was all together now; there were no more parts on the ground. It was bright red and it didn't look bad at all.

Bob and Short Stuff closed the hood and got in the front seat.

"Jamie, Bobby," Dick called, "I'm going to back down the driveway. Do you want a ride?"

"Yes, yes." Bobby and Jamie scrambled into the back seat. "Come on, Katie. Can Katie come too?"

"Sure. Come on, Katie," Dick called, starting up the motor.

Katie squeezed in with the small boys, and Dick backed cautiously down the driveway. When he reached the sidewalk he tooted the horn twice and everybody climbed out of the car. Then Bob and Short Stuff pushed the car back up the driveway again.

Katie smiled to herself as the car inched slowly toward the backyard. Well, at least she'd had a sort of ride in it. But would it ever go forward?

The little boys followed the car back and Katie returned to the front steps.

The next few days brought several prospects to Mr. Johnson's house. Late one afternoon when Katie was helping her mother fix dinner the telephone rang. Mrs. Hart picked up the phone in the hall, and motioned to Katie to go listen on the extension. Katie hurried up the stairs and into her parents' room. She picked up the receiver and listened.

"They're awfully nice people," a woman's voice on the other end was saying. "They heard through a friend of theirs about Katie's letter, and they're coming out from the city this weekend to look at the house."

"That's nice," Mrs. Hart was saying graciously, and then the other voice went on:

"They've called me twice long distance to talk about the house. They sound very interested."

"Who are they?" Mrs. Hart asked.

"Mr. and Mrs. Wentworth," the real estate broker said. "Such lovely people," she cooed.

"Do they have any children?" Mrs. Hart asked.

"Yes, one. That's the idea. They want to get this one child of theirs out of the city."

Katie could hardly keep from speaking, she longed so to ask about "the child."

"Do they have a boy or a girl?" Mrs. Hart asked. "And how old?"

"Well, now, I don't remember," the woman said. "I think she said her daughter but, oh dear, maybe she didn't. We have so many people looking at houses, I can't recall all the details." She laughed lightly. "I'm afraid I just can't remember."

It's maddening, Katie thought, gripping the telephone tightly and putting her hand over the mouthpiece.

Mrs. Hart thanked the woman for calling and then waited until she hung up.

"Katie," her mother said into the phone, "are you still there?"

"Yes," Katie said woefully. "If only she could remember."

"Well, don't give up hope," her mother said soothingly. "Come down and set the table now, dear."

Katie smiled into the phone at her mother. Nice Mom. She knew how Katie felt. She understood.

Katie sat on the edge of the bed, staring out the window at the fluttering green leaves on the tree outside the window. The sun had clouded over and it looked like rain. She counted the days until the weekend. This was Wednesday. It wouldn't be long.

The Lonely Only

Saturday came at last. It was one of those clear, sparkling days. It had rained off and on since Wednesday, and now everything — trees, sky, grass, and sidewalks — looked washed and clean.

As Katie closed her window that morning she shivered from the early morning chill. She dressed quickly trying hard not to think about the people who were coming today. No use in worrying about it, she told herself severely. Anyway, school would be starting again soon and she would see her friends every day.

Katie put on her favorite jeans, a high-necked yellow sweater, and her sneakers. She started to comb her hair carefully, then threw down the comb. It was no use. She was just too excited to fuss. Wonder when they'll come, she thought, as she hurried downstairs.

Katie was surprised to find her mother was already in the kitchen. She had a dressed-up look about her for a Saturday morning. She was busy at the stove, and smiled as Katie came into the room. Without even being asked, Katie began to set the table in the dining room. She put out the forks and then went to look out the window. She got the knives and then looked out the window again. Will they ever come? she wondered as she went back to get out the spoons.

Twice during breakfast Katie found some excuse to go to the kitchen, so that she could peek out the window at the Johnson house.

Right after breakfast, just as though she'd been waiting for the Harts to get up from the table, Sarah Lou called. She told Katie excitedly that she and Jody were going to attend Miss Rumsey's dancing school in the fall. They were going to wear matching blue dresses with the same color gloves and shoes. In a way, Katie wished Sarah Lou wouldn't call her every time she and Jody decided to do something together. It gave her a left-out feeling. But it was better than not knowing at all.

"And, you know, we'll have to dance with boys," Sarah Lou giggled. "Mom's going to fix my hair for me. So I'll have lots of partners, she said. By the way, Katie, are you going?"

"I don't know," Katie said doubtfully. "I'll have to ask Mother. I hope she'll let me go. It would be fun, Sarah Lou." Then Katie suddenly remembered about the people coming next door.

"Oh, Sarah Lou!" she exclaimed in a burst of excitement. "Guess what?" Katie told Sarah Lou all she knew about the Wentworths.

Finally, when she hung up and hurried to the window, she saw a car parked in front of Mr. Johnson's house. Katie dashed out the front door, but there wasn't a person in sight. Oh, why had she talked so long?

Katie walked across the lawn and climbed on the logs stacked against the wall of Mr. Johnson's garden. Suddenly a voice sounded above her. "Hello, there." Katie looked around. "I'm up here," the voice called. Katie saw a girl sitting up high among the branches of an old apple tree that grew at the back of Mr. Johnson's garden.

Katie stared in surprise.

"Why don't you come up?" the girl said.

"Are you . . . uh . . . are your parents looking at this house?" Katie asked.

"Oh, yes," the girl said happily. "I think they're going to buy it."

"You do!" Katie exclaimed. She tried to smother the burst of hope inside her.

"Yes." The girl smiled down at Katie. "My name is Jo Ann Wentworth. We live in the city. Is it nice here?"

"Oh, yes," Katie said eagerly. "And it would be even nicer if you moved here," she added. "Have you been in the house yet?"

"Oh, yes," Jo Ann smiled. "It's very nice. I've got my room all picked out and my mother's already planning where the furniture will go. My dad likes it too. He heard about your letter from some friends at work and he said that Apple Street sounds like a good neighborhood for us."

"He did?" Katie beamed.

"Yes," Jo Ann nodded. "I'm a lonely only, you see."

"A what?" Katie asked, startled.

"A lonely only," Jo Ann laughed. "You know, an only child — no brothers and no sisters."

"Oh." Katie couldn't think what to say to that.

"Could you show me your house?" Jo Ann asked shyly.

"Of course, I'd love to." Katie smiled. "Come on down. There's a gate in the wall there," Katie said pointing. "You can come through that way."

Jo Ann jumped down quickly, and when she stood on the Harts' lawn Katie saw that she was only a little bit taller than herself. She had short blond hair and she wore a pair of black corduroy jeans. Katie decided right then to ask her mother to get her a pair just like them.

"What grade are you in?" Katie asked. To her

delight Jo Ann said, "Going into sixth. That's the same as you, isn't it?"

Katie could hardly believe her ears. Here was a girl, about to move in next door, and she was in the same grade. It was too wonderful. She was almost afraid to count on it, for fear there'd be some last-minute hitch.

As they went up the steps of her house, Katie was sure she saw her mother peeping out at them through the kitchen curtains. Poor Mom, she must be excited too, Katie realized.

But when the girls entered the house, Mrs. Hart was busy arranging china in the dining room cupboard. She had a happy look about her, though.

"It's so nice to meet you," she said after Katie had introduced Jo Ann. "Are your folks buying the house?" Katie could tell she was trying to sound casual. She smiled when Jo Ann said she thought so.

Katie showed Jo Ann over the downstairs and then took her up to her room. She showed her her jewelry and her figurines. Jo Ann admired everything. She said she must get some glass horses just like Katie's. Katie felt sure they could become good friends. While they were in the room, Jamie came charging up the stairs and stopped in the doorway.

"Hi," he said loudly. "Are you the new girl? Mom says you might buy Mr. Johnson's house."

"Hi," said Jo Ann, looking at him with a smile. "I'm pretty sure we will."

"That's good," Jamie said enthusiastically. "Katie sure needs a friend."

Jo Ann just laughed, and Katie said in her most grown-up voice, "This is my brother, Jamie."

"And this is Wilbur," Jamie said, holding out the box toward Jo Ann. "He's a toad."

"Oh, yes," Jo Ann said solemnly, bending over the box.

"Would you like to hold him?" Jamie asked eagerly.

Jo Ann didn't giggle or back away. She just said, "I'd love to." When Jamie handed her the toad, she cradled it gently in her hands for a minute.

Katie could tell she'd made a big hit with Jamie. He took her down the hall to see his room. Jo Ann examined the baseball pictures on the wall, the bottle of dead ladybugs, and Jamie's rocks.

Then they went out in the yard to see Katie's garden and Dick's car. While they were standing there looking at the garden, Will came up the driveway. When Katie told him Jo Ann might move in next door, she thought he'd moan or groan or do something silly. But he surprised her by saying, "That's great! Katie gets kind of tired of all the boys on Apple Street. She needs more friends."

Katie wished everyone would stop making her

sound so desperate for friends. "I have lots of friends at school," she said proudly.

"Yes," grinned Will, "but we have to keep Katie out of trouble at home."

Out of trouble — keep her out of trouble! Of all the nerve. Katie began to feel cross.

"Look who's talking," she retorted, with a toss of her head. "You're lucky you won't have to live right next door to him," she said, turning to Jo Ann.

"Like to sit in my brother's car?" Jamie asked, hoping to stop an argument.

"Someday it's going to run," Will said, "but we still have some work to do on it."

"It's very nice," Jo Ann said with a sparkle in her eyes. She even admired the engine when Will raised the hood for her. They then heard Jo Ann's mother calling her.

"Come, walk to the car with me," Jo Ann said, slipping her arm around Katie's waist.

"Oh, Jo Ann, I hope you *will* move in," Katie said. "We'd have so much fun. We could play up in my room, or if the boys pester us we could go play at your house."

Katie was worried suddenly that Jo Ann might not want to play at her house. Being an only child, she might be used to having everything quiet and just the way she wanted it at home.

"Oh, I hope so too," Jo Ann assured her. "It's

89

so quiet when I go home. There's never anybody to talk to or laugh with except Mother. It'll be lots of fun to play at your house, maybe even more fun than at my house."

"Really?" Katie was delighted but startled. Imagine a girl thinking a house full of boys would be more fun.

She watched Jo Ann and her mother and father drive away with the real estate agent. She waved until they were out of sight, then she whirled around and raced into the house.

"Isn't it wonderful, Mom?" Katie exclaimed happily. She threw her arms around her mother and jumped up and down. "Oh, I'm so happy."

"Katie, stop." Her mother laughed. "You're jumping on my toes. It is wonderful, but it isn't absolutely certain yet. There'll be a mortgage to arrange, and lots of other matters."

"Oh, but it will work out, I know. I have to call Sarah Lou. I have to tell her all about Jo Ann. Oh, by the way, Mom, am I going to dancing school this year?"

"Yes indeed," Mrs. Hart said, "in just a few weeks."

"Maybe Jo Ann could go too," Katie said, practically dancing her way to the phone. "I'll have to tell Sarah Lou that too."

Miss Rumsey's Dancing School

It was the middle of October before the Wentworths finally moved into Mr. Johnson's house. School had started, and the long summer days were over. The first two days after Jo Ann arrived, she and Katie were together every minute. Katie hadn't even had a chance to call Sarah Lou, she'd been so busy. There were a million things she and Jo Ann needed to tell each other, or do together.

The very first evening of the day Jo Ann moved in, the boys were playing touch football in front of Will's house. Jo Ann and Katie sat on the front steps watching.

When the boys suddenly invited them into the game, Jo Ann whispered, "Let's Katie. It looks like fun." Jo Ann looked so eager, Katie agreed. It was fun, although Will was always right beside Katie to tap her out everytime she got the ball. When it was over Jo Ann told Katie she'd never had so much fun.

The days passed happily, and then came the Saturday of Miss Rumsey's first dancing class. Katie was nervous and not at all sure she wanted to go. But at least Jo Ann was going too.

"I suppose I'll dance with boys," Katie said to her mother, who was ironing in the kitchen.

"Of course, dear," Mrs. Hart said.

"What should I wear?" Katie asked.

"I thought you might like to wear your pink dress," Mrs. Hart replied, "so I pressed it." She took the dress off the back of the door and handed it to Katie. The skirt was full and there were tiny red flowers embroidered around the neckline.

"And you can wear your red shoes with it," Mrs. Hart said.

Katie began to get excited as she thought of dressing for the dance. She could just see herself swirling around the room. But she'd have to dance with someone, that was the trouble. Who would her partner be? Who would ask her?

"The boys will step all over my shoes," she said, looking for some excuse to back out.

Her mother laughed. "You'll just have to put up with that. It will be fun, Katie, you'll see."

"Will Dick take me?" Katie asked.

Mrs. Hart frowned a little as she said, "No, he's busy with his car."

Lately whenever Dick's name was mentioned Katie's mother looked worried. Dick had gotten his driver's license and though he did drive the family car, his own rattletrap, as his mother called his car, didn't run yet.

At lunchtime Dick came in covered with grease. Jamie trailed in after him.

"It's not running yet," Jamie announced cheerfully.

"Think it'll ever run, Dick?" Katie asked.

Katie alternated between siding with her mother, who said she wished the old thing would never run, and hoping it would run so she could ride in it. She supposed her father was right when he said, "It's a good experience for the boy. He's got to grow up sometime."

Mrs. Hart seemed to think Dick would turn into a wild-eyed speed demon the minute he stepped into his own car.

"I think it's just about ready," Dick said confidently. "Want a ride, Mom?"

Mrs. Hart sighed. "Maybe some time. Remember, you have to drive an old car more carefully."

"I know, Mom," Dick grinned. "You've told me that about a thousand times." He got up from the lunch table and patted his mother's shoulder. "I'll be okay, Mom, honest."

After lunch Katie got dressed. She took a long time brushing and combing her hair. When she was all ready, she looked at herself in the mirror. She did look older, and taller, she was sure of it.

At two o'clock that afternoon Katie and Jo Ann met Jody and Sarah Lou in the large mirrored room of Miss Rumsey's dancing school. Will and Short Stuff and several other boys and girls from their class were standing around the room talking quietly. They all looked slightly uncomfortable in their best clothes. They were used to sneakers and blue jeans. As Katie listened to Miss Rumsey's instructions, she thought her friends looked very grownup in their light dresses and dark suits.

"Now, attention," Miss Rumsey said loudly and tapped on the floor with a long thin cane. She started to demonstrate a dance step. "Now, follow," she called over her shoulder. The boys and girls scuffed along after her. Katie resisted a strong impulse to giggle.

After a few minutes Miss Rumsey rapped again with the cane. "Now, class, we will dance with partners. Will each boy please choose a girl to dance with?"

The boys shuffled uncertainly and the girls smiled nervously.

"Come, come," Miss Rumsey called. "Pick a girl quickly and ask her properly."

Suddenly there was Will standing in front of Katie. His hair was neatly combed, and his face had turned a bright red color. Will scraped his feet and looked miserable. Katie thought he looked as if he had a stomachache.

"Hi, Will," she said.

Will's blush grew brighter and he couldn't seem to talk.

"Are you asking me to dance?" Katie said quietly. Somehow she'd known all along it would be Will who would ask her.

"Yes," Will blurted out. Katie suddenly felt sorry for him, sorry for old freckle-nose, Will Madison. She remembered that whenever Jamie was hurt or upset about something she would talk away like mad to take his mind off it. So, to make Will feel at ease, she said, "Did you know Dick's almost got his car fixed?"

"Say, that's great!" Will exclaimed. "I sure hope he gives me a ride right away." The pink in his face had begun to fade.

"You know, I think Jamie hopes he'll go on working on that car forever," Katie laughed. Will laughed too, and he looked almost normal. "Jamie follows Dick around all the time now," Katie chatted on, and in a minute the music started.

Will stepped on her shoes, but Katie remembered what her mother had said. Will, who could move so smoothly on a ball field, stumbled across the dance floor, and Katie tried to follow. When Dick had taught her to waltz and fox trot, he'd said it was important for the girl to follow, to go where the boy went instead of struggling off in a different direction. She thought they'd dance better to rock music, but that wasn't Miss Rumsey's kind of dancing.

"Boy!" exclaimed Will after a minute. "I'm awful."

"No, you're not," Katie said. "It takes a little practice. You'll be as good as Dick soon."

Since Dick was in high school, Will looked gratified.

"Do you think so?" he said.

They danced by a corner of the room, where the girls were dancing with one another. There were never enough boys at Miss Rumsey's classes, and the girls who didn't get picked by a boy had to dance with one another. Jody was one of those girls, but she smiled brightly as Katie and Will went past. Katie caught a glimpse of Jo Ann dancing with Short Stuff at the far end of the room, and Katie was glad she too had a boy for a partner.

When the dance ended, Will said thank you and quickly joined the circle of boys again. Miss Rumsey again stood in front of the class and demonstrated another dance step. Then Miss Rumsey again told the boys to choose partners. Katie stood uncertainly, wondering whether to hope for another partner or to head for the corner where all the girls danced together.

Then Katie heard her name called, and there was Short Stuff hurrying toward her. "May I have this dance?" he asked. "Say, listen," he said, not waiting for an answer, "how'd Dick make out with his car this morning? Is he going to drive it today?"

"Why, I don't — "

"What about the manifold?" Short Stuff asked.

"Hi," said Will, coming up to them. "Is Katie . . . ?"

"Yes, she's dancing with me," Short Stuff said. "Why don't you go find Jo Ann or somebody? Katie says maybe Dick's gonna drive his car this afternoon and the manifold is fixed."

"I did!" Katie exclaimed, but the music had started and no one heard her.

"Come on, let's get this over with." Short Stuff took an iron grip on her hand and stepped on her shoes. Katie winced and set off valiantly. This wasn't quite the way she had thought people danced on a ballroom floor, but at least they were covering a lot of ground.

"That's great news about the manifold," Short Stuff shouted in her ear, and Katie decided it was simpler just to nod and say, "Yes, isn't it?"

After a few more rounds Katie said, "Dancing is kind of fun, don't you think?"

Short Stuff reddened slightly. "Yeah, it's okay. I don't mind dancing with you or Jo Ann."

The music ended then and Miss Rumsey announced a brief intermission. "And no dividing up," she ordered. "For five minutes you boys and girls are to chat with one another as though you were at a formal dance."

"Guess we'll have to keep on talking," Short Stuff grinned. "Do you mind, Katie?"

"Of course not," Katie said happily.

"Where'd Jamie ever get that toad, anyway?" Short Stuff asked. They talked and laughed about Wilbur some more. Then Short Stuff said that the new girl, Jo Ann, was a lot of fun. She'd laughed when he'd ask her if she'd seen any ghosts in her house, and laughed even more when he'd told her about Will's trick and how Katie had gotten even. And Katie, remembering all that, found that she herself was laughing so much that she was surprised when the music started again and Miss Rumsey ordered them to change partners.

When the next dance started, a boy Katie didn't know came up to her. He looked as ill at ease as Will had. But even though Katie didn't know him, she thought he looked slightly familiar.

"May I have this dance?" he mumbled. Katie was beginning to enjoy having a new partner every time. She smiled and said, "Thank you." Then, since the boy didn't seem to know what to say next, she said, "Do you have any pets? My brother has a toad."

"Ah . . . no . . . but I used to. My name's Phillip Bates and I just started in school here this week."

The red color in his face began to fade as he talked.

"Ready, begin," called Miss Rumsey.

After that dance Miss Rumsey announced that the girls were to choose partners this time. Katie stood wondering what do do. Across the room she saw Jo Ann turn to Short Stuff. Katie looked around quickly to see if there was anyone she knew standing near her. She saw that Sarah Lou and Jody too had partners. Oh dear, what should she do?

Then out of the corner of her eye she saw Will edging toward her, trying to look very casual. Several girls were hurrying in his direction, so Katie stepped up to him quickly.

"Will, may I have this dance?" she asked. Will's face turned pink again.

"Oh hi, Katie," he said. "Why, sure, I didn't see you standing there."

When the class was over, Katie and Jo Ann, Sarah Lou and Jody chatted about the dance as they got their coats.

"Wasn't it awful?" giggled Sarah Lou. "I had to dance with two boys in my class."

"Too bad about you," Jody laughed.

"Look at my poor shoes," moaned Katie. "All those boys stepping on them."

"How many did you dance with?" Jody asked.

"I forget how many," Katie said contentedly.

"Anyway, we all got to dance with boys, and there weren't too many — boys, I mean. I saw you dancing a lot too, Jo Ann," she added.

"Yes," Jo Ann said, "everyone is so nice, but I was glad I knew a few of the boys from Apple Street."

It was late afternoon as they all came out of the building. There was a long line of cars drawn up waiting for some of the pupils, while others began to walk home. Katie and Jo Ann started down the steps, then they saw it — Dick's car driving right along and going forward too.

"Dick!" Katie shrieked. Dick pulled the car up to the curb, and Katie could see Jamie on the back seat.

"Hello, Katie," Dick called. "I came to give you a ride home."

Katie grabbed Jo Ann's hand and pulled her along, down the steps and across the sidewalk.

"Dick, how wonderful! You got it going."

"Hey, Dick," Short Stuff and Will called from down the street. "Wait for us."

"Okay," Dick grinned. "Climb in, everybody. Yes, you too, Jo Ann. Hurry! We're holding up traffic."

They all squeezed into the car — Katie and Jo Ann on the back seat with Jamie, Short Stuff and Will up front with Dick. Dick tooted the horn, and Katie waved to the girls, who stood on the sidewalk staring at them enviously.

As the car started, Will turned around and flicked a rubber band at Katie, and Katie just picked it up and flicked it right back at him. She decided she had never been so happy.

About the Author

MARTHA TOLLES is the author of two other Apple Paperbacks about Katie, *Katie's Baby-sitting Job* and *Katie for President*. She has also written *Who's Reading Darci's Diary?* and *Darci and the Dance Contest*.

A graduate of Smith College, Mrs. Tolles lives with her husband in San Marino, California.

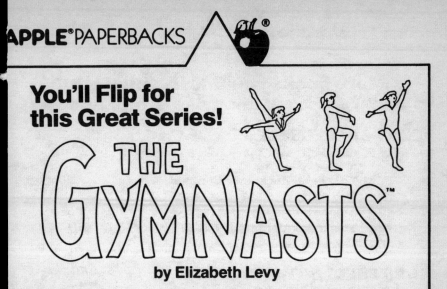

APPLE®PAPERBACKS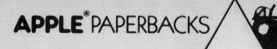

More books you'll love, filled with mystery, adventure, friendship, and fun!

NEW APPLE TITLES

☐ 40388-5	**Cassie Bowen Takes Witch Lessons** Anna Grossnickle Hines		**$2.50**
☐ 33824-2	**Darci and the Dance Contest**	Martha Tolles	**$2.50**
☐ 40494-6	**The Little Gymnast**	Sheila Haigh	**$2.50**
☐ 40403-2	**A Secret Friend**	Marilyn Sachs	**$2.50**
☐ 40402-4	**The Truth About Mary Rose**	Marilyn Sachs	**$2.50**
☐ 40405-9	**Veronica Ganz**	Marilyn Sachs	**$2.50**

BEST-SELLING APPLE TITLES

☐ 33662-2	**Dede Takes Charge!**	Johanna Hurwitz	**$2.50**
☐ 41042-3	**The Dollhouse Murders**	Betty Ren Wright	**$2.50**
☐ 40755-4	**Ghosts Beneath Our Feet**	Betty Ren Wright	**$2.50**
☐ 40950-6	**The Girl With the Silver Eyes**	Willo Davis Roberts	**$2.50**
☐ 40605-1	**Help! I'm a Prisoner in the Library**	Eth Clifford	**$2.50**
☐ 40724-4	**Katie's Baby-sitting Job**	Martha Tolles	**$2.50**
☐ 40725-2	**Nothing's Fair in Fifth Grade**	Barthe DeClements	**$2.50**
☐ 40382-6	**Oh Honestly, Angela!**	Nancy K. Robinson	**$2.50**
☐ 33894-3	**The Secret of NIMH**	Robert C. O'Brien	**$2.25**
☐ 40180-7	**Sixth Grade Can Really Kill You** Barthe DeClements		**$2.50**
☐ 40874-7	**Stage Fright**	Ann M. Martin	**$2.50**
☐ 40305-2	**Veronica the Show-off**	Nancy K. Robinson	**$2.50**
☐ 41224-8	**Who's Reading Darci's Diary?**	Martha Tolles	**$2.50**
☐ 41119-5	**Yours Till Niagara Falls, Abby**	Jane O'Connor	**$2.50**

Available wherever you buy books...or use the coupon below.